# Silvertip

## A Year in the Life of a Yellowstone Grizzly

### Ted Rechlin

RIVERBEND
PUBLISHING

## DEDICATION

*This book is dedicated to the Grizzly, the King of Yellowstone.*

### ABOUT THE ARTIST/AUTHOR

Ted Rechlin has worked professionally in picture book illustration, comic book art, trading cards, graphic design, and tattoo design.

Most of Ted's time is spent at the drawing board, working on illustration projects, or teaching his craft to aspiring artists.

When Ted's not working at his Bozeman, Montana, home, he can usually be found hiking the Yellowstone backcountry.

For more information on Ted's art, teaching, and appearances, visit www.tedrechlinart.com.

*Silvertip: A Year in the Life of a Yellowstone Grizzly*
Copyright © 2011 by Ted Rechlin

Published by Riverbend Publishing, Helena, Montana

ISBN 13: 978-1-60639-034-4

2 3 4 5 6 7 8 9 0 EP 18 17 16 15 14 13

Design by DD Dowden

RIVERBEND PUBLISHING
P.O. Box 5833
Helena, MT 59604
1-866-787-2363
www.riverbendpublishing.com

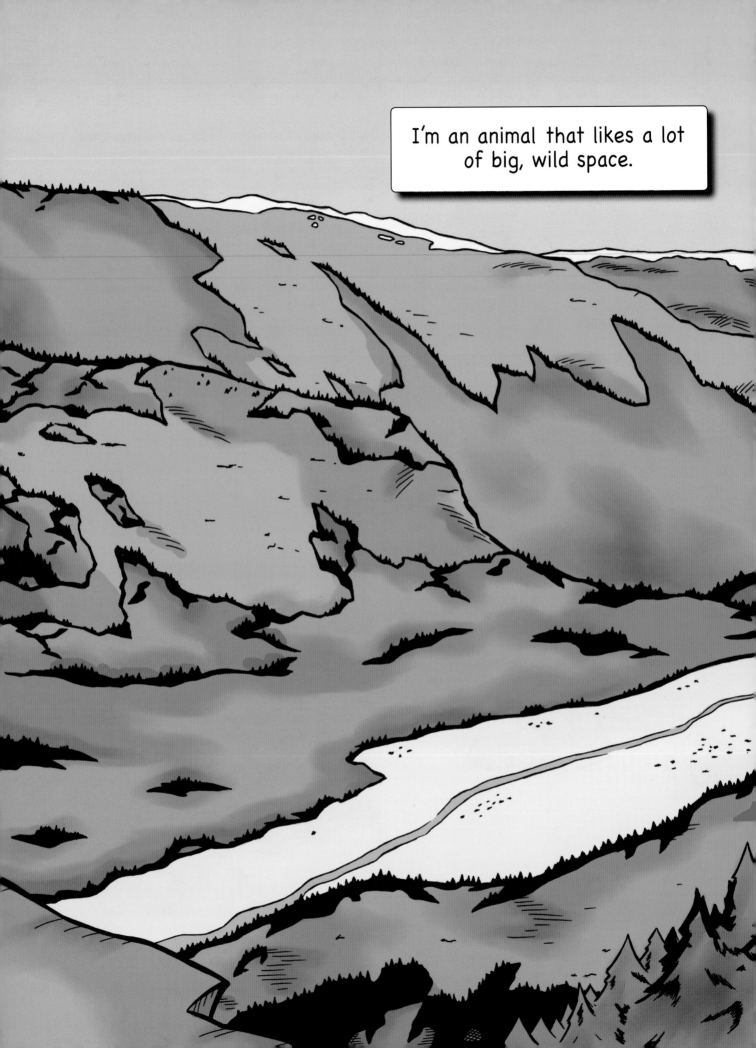

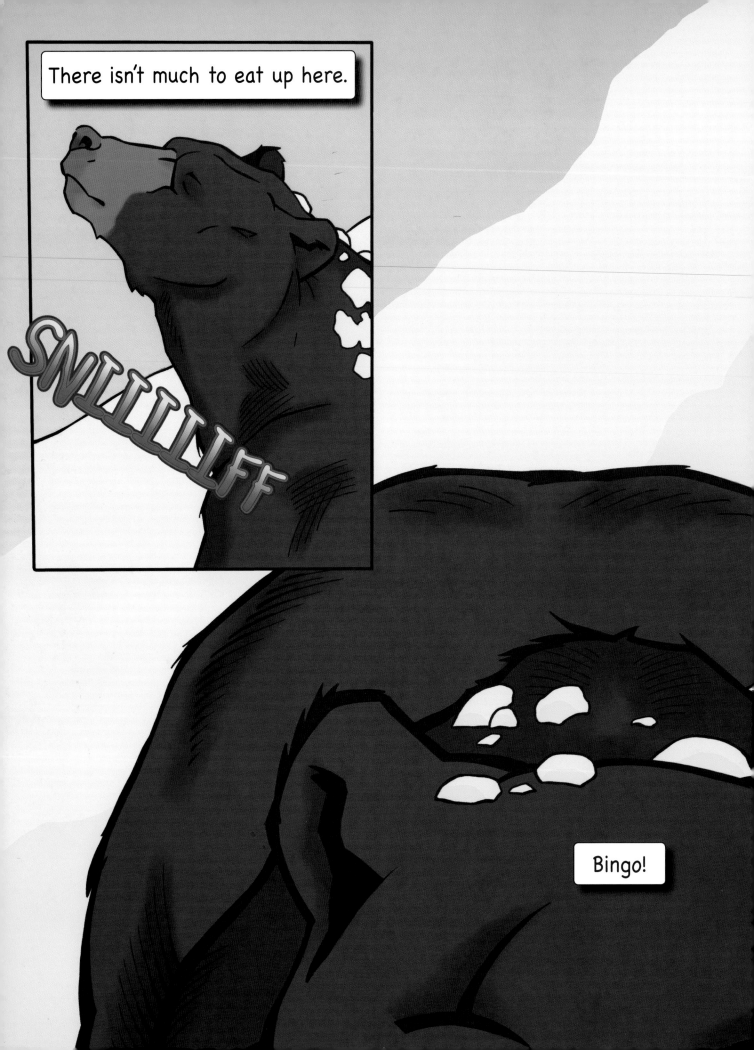

In the fall I'm always hungrier than ever and it always feels like there isn't enough to eat.

The fight is mostly a blur.

What happened?